Jennifer —

MW00940778

THE CROW'S GIFT
AND OTHER TALES

BY
SONORA TAYLOR *Sy '21*

Thank you!

Sonora Taylor

The Crow's Gift and Other Tales by Sonora Taylor

© 2017 Sonora Taylor

All rights reserved. No portion of this book may be reproduced in any form without permission from the author.

For more information, visit the author's website at sonorawrites.com

This is a work of fiction. Names, characters, places, and incidents are the products of the author's imagination. Any resemblance to actual persons, living or dead, events, or locales is entirely coincidental.

Cover art by Doug Puller.

To Will

TABLE OF CONTENTS

THE CROW'S GIFT

Tabitha loved the variety of birds she saw every morning on her walk to school. Now in 4th grade, she walked alone; however, as a small child, her mother had walked with her and taught her how to name each bird she saw along the way: sparrows, blue jays, wrens and robins. They hid in trees and danced on the gravel. They picked up worms from rain-soaked sidewalks and shared the branches with foraging squirrels. Her walk to school would've been lonely now if it weren't for the birds. She loved their company, and she loved them all — even the crows.

The crows were different from the others. She'd see them in groups, but only with each other. They stayed atop telephone phones, or tucked into trees with no other birds or creatures. Perhaps they liked to be left alone. Or maybe they wanted friends, and the other animals kept them away.

Tabitha knew how that felt. Her classmate Jane sometimes had space for her at the lunch table. And many children quietly agreed if she asked to play. But no one asked her to play with them. No one sat at her table at lunch. No one invited her to their house after school.

No one actually wanted to be her friend.

Tabitha thus felt sorry for the lonely crows, and tried her best to be their friend. When she walked past them, she'd wave and say, "Hello!" She suspected the crows didn't speak English, but it was her hope that they knew, in their own way, that she was greeting them. That she was acknowledging them, and saw them as friends.

Her efforts were rewarded one morning when a silent crow suddenly squawked as she walked by.

Tabitha felt a rush of excitement, but brushed it off. It was a bird — birds made noise. She still greeted him. "Hello!" she said, waving.

Two squawks this time, and a flap of his wings.

It couldn't be. Could it?

Tabitha smiled all the rest of the way to school. Even if it was just pretend, it was nice to think that she had made a new friend.

"Hey look, it's Terrible Tabitha."

Simon's taunts were mean, but not very creative. Creativity required intelligence. As usual, Tabitha kept her eyes averted in an attempt to ignore him, and his horrible friends who snickered at his every word.

Most of the children left Tabitha alone. But not Simon. Tabitha didn't know when or why Simon had chosen to be mean to her. Most days she could ignore him, but that didn't stop the gnawing sadness that grew when she saw him at school. His torment had grown out of nowhere. Now it was so ingrained in their routine that she simply saw it as something true, like the sun rising each morning or the birds migrating each winter.

Simon always started the day by finding something about her to mock — usually her secondhand clothes, or her large glasses, or her flat pale hair, or the small amount of pudge around her middle. He cycled through them in such a pattern that she wondered if he had a collection of socks with different "Insults for Tabitha" stitched on them for each day.

Today it was clothing. "Where did those pants come from? Goodwill's reject pile?" More laughter. Tabitha kept her back to them, wishing she could stop the slow flush rising up her cheeks. She was saved by the arrival of their teacher, Miss Patterson. Simon was cruel and stupid, but not enough of either to bully Tabitha in front of a teacher.

The school day passed as normal, including more mockery from Simon at lunch. Rather than listen to his taunts, she'd sequestered herself in the library, leaving her lunch unfinished and her mind preoccupied with shame and loneliness. Her distraction remained during her lessons, making the hours pass all the more slowly. The final bell rang like music in her ears, and she walked home, shuddering against the growing chill in the wind.

She gathered rocks as she walked, the stones ranging from mundane to beautiful. She liked decorating her windowsill with them. As she pocketed her gathered stones, she noticed one of the crows standing on a fence post.

"Hello!" she said, waving her fingers.

Squawk! A flap of his wings. Surely that was an answer — it wasn't possible that could happen twice. She smiled. Maybe she did have a new friend.

Tabitha remembered some uneaten crackers in her lunchbox. "Are you hungry?" she asked. The crow didn't squawk or flap, but stood still, watching her. She reached into her lunchbox and pulled out a cracker. Still seeing no response from the crow, she placed it on the ground slowly.

Squawk! As she backed away, the crow swooped down onto the cracker, grabbing it and returning to his post in a single loop. He swallowed the cracker, flapped his wings, and squawked again. Then he flew away.

Tabitha smiled. Even though it was brief, and with a bird, it was nice to have a friendly interaction that day. She left three whole crackers in a line on the post, in case the crow or his group returned. In her mind, she named him Timothy.

Tabitha and her mother lived in an unremarkable home, a single story surrounded by a barren lawn. It's what they could afford. Tabitha never knew her father. She used to ask her mother about him, but she only received clipped answers and teary eyes. She couldn't help but wonder if those conversations were one of the reasons her mother stopped walking with her to school. She learned to make it a point not to upset her, if that's what it took to keep her close.

Despite her best efforts, though, Tabitha often saw how sad her mother was. Today was no exception. Tabitha saw her mother cooking, occasionally wiping her eyes between stirring the pot. She watched her mother silently, not wanting to disturb her. She knew it embarrassed her mother when Tabitha saw her cry, and Tabitha didn't want to sadden her further. After watching her for a few moments, she turned back around the corner, leaning against the wall and listening for signs that dinner would be ready soon.

"Tabitha!" her mother called. She heard the skillet start to sizzle, bowls clinking onto the counter. "Come set the table, please."

She scurried into the kitchen, and her mother, red-eyed but otherwise appearing all right, laughed with a start. "Right there!" she exclaimed. "Were you outside the kitchen the whole time?"

"I'd just come near the door," Tabitha lied.

Her mother smiled. "My little ghost." Tabitha grinned. She looked at the counter and saw dinner. Grilled cheese and soup — one of her favorites. Her mother saw it as basic food, poor food, but Tabitha loved it.

"Put the bowls and plates on the table, please," her mother said. "The sandwiches are almost done."

Tabitha did as she was told, placing everything perfectly. She didn't want to spill soup or leave any spoons askew on the napkin. A nice table usually made her mother smile.

No sooner had she sat in her chair than her mother turned off the oven and carried a hot skillet of fresh sandwiches to the table. Tabitha watched hungrily as the sandwiches slid onto their plates. She immediately tucked into her sandwich, not bothering to wait for it to cool.

"How was school today, darling?" her mother asked, slowly sipping her soup.

"It was fine." She talked a bit about some of her lessons. Tabitha usually left her school stories short. She didn't want to trouble her mother with stories about Simon. Her mother listened quietly, sipping soup and giving an occasional "Mm hmm." Tabitha knew her mind was elsewhere, on whatever had been making her cry before.

She wondered if hearing about the crows would cheer her mother up. "I also made a new animal friend after school today."

Her mother looked up. "A new animal friend?"

"Yes," Tabitha said, "a crow. A big black one, with shiny wings. I've named him Timothy."

"Timothy," her mother replied. "A strong name."

"Yes." Tabitha was glad to see her mother was interested. "I said hello, and he squawked at me. He even flapped his wings, like he was waving at me."

"Crows are very intelligent birds. I bet he recognized you."

"That's what I thought! And I saw him after school, and gave him a cracker. He squawked again and ate it and then flew away, so I left three more for him and his friends."

"Be careful feeding them, Tabitha." Her mother's face grew serious. "That was very nice, but he could've bitten or scratched you."

Tabitha's face flushed. She'd been trying to cheer her mother up, and instead made her worry. "I was careful," she said, her eyes cast down on her plate. "I put the crackers on the ground first."

"Oh. That's good, then. You're a smart little girl."

Tabitha smiled. All was well.

"You mentioned Timothy and his friends," her mother said, sipping her water. "Do you know what a group of crows is called?"

"Just a group, right?" Tabitha asked.

"No. Something more sinister." Her mother smiled slyly. "They're called a murder of crows."

"A murder!" Tabitha's eyes widened in shock, yet she couldn't help but grin with glee. A murder sounded so forbidden.

"That's right." Her mother dabbed her mouth with a napkin, her soup gone and her sandwich mostly finished. "Crows are quite friendly, as you saw today. But make sure you're friendly to them. They remember kindness, but they also don't forget cruelty — just like people."

Tabitha nodded. "I would never hurt them," she declared. "Timothy's my friend. I'd never hurt him or his friends."

Her mother patted her hand. "And I'm sure they'll never hurt you. Kindness speaks volumes." She turned from Tabitha and looked out the window, seeing everything but what was outside. Tabitha's shoulders fell. Despite her best efforts, she'd lost her mother yet again.

"I'll clear the table," Tabitha said, wishing that people had been kinder to her mother.

The next morning, Tabitha walked to school with the most happiness she'd felt since she started walking alone. She hoped to see Timothy and the rest of his murder. Hopefully the growing cold hadn't scared him away. Did crows fly away for the winter?

If so, then they hadn't left yet. When Tabitha rounded the corner, walking near the old fence post, she heard a loud squawk. She looked at the tree it had come from, delight crossing her face.

"Good morning, Timothy," Tabitha called, waving.

Squawk! He flapped his wings this time. Tabitha thought for sure he was waving. He flew across her, landed on the fence post, and let out another loud squawk, pointing his beak at the post. Was he beckoning her?

Tabitha walked to the post, and Timothy took flight; but only to a nearby branch. She gasped when she looked at the post. Lying upon it were three colorful stones, neatly polished. They looked like the stones she collected, but nicer, less blemished. She bet he'd found them far off in the woods, somewhere only an animal would think to look.

"They're beautiful!" she exclaimed. She quickly pocketed them, and looked at Timothy in gratitude. He cocked his head at her. "Thank you!" she cried, waving.

Squawk! He took flight, soaring into the thickest trees. Tabitha stuffed her hands into her pockets, keeping the stones pressed against her fingers. She vowed to pocket more of her crackers during lunch.

"All right class." The lights went out, and voices hushed. "Please direct your attention to the board."

Tabitha normally did this, but not today. She was too distracted. A crow had brought her a gift. In just 24 hours, a bird had shown her more kindness than her classmates had shown her all year.

"Today," Miss Patterson continued, "we'll be learning about birds."

This brought Tabitha's attention back to the board. On the wall, she saw a projection of an assortment of birds. Miss Patterson clicked through, and an albatross came up. "Who can tell me what this bird is?"

"Albatross," the class recited, and Tabitha continued to only listen with half an ear. She guessed Miss Patterson would go through the birds alphabetically. Sure enough, a short time later she heard the class answer, "Bluebird." She doodled in her notebook.

However, upon hearing "Crow," she looked straight up. A painted picture of a crow stood in front of her. It looked small compared to Timothy.

"Yes, a crow," Miss Patterson said. "Not to be confused with a raven — crows are much smaller." Tabitha didn't think Timothy was as big as a raven, but he did have a good size to his feathers. Maybe the crow on the board was a girl.

"Can anyone tell me what they know about crows?" Miss Patterson asked.

Multiple hands shot up, including Tabitha's. Tabitha normally preferred to hide her answers from Miss Patterson's attention and Simon's taunts; but seeing the crow — an image of her friend — made her feel brave.

Miss Patterson, however, saw her other classmates first. She pointed at various students, who answered with the basics. "They're black!" said Susan. "They eat dead things!" said Jason. "They travel in groups!" said Jane.

"They're not called groups!" Tabitha shouted. She knew she'd spoken out of turn, but she was too excited to care. Miss Patterson turned in her direction, her eyes wide. "A group of crows is called a murder."

"Very good, Tabitha," Miss Patterson said, her look of shock becoming pleasant surprise. "She's right. A flock of crows is called a murder."

Tabitha beamed, proud to be praised in front of her classmates. "They're also very intelligent," she continued, unable to stop herself. "They recognize people. They know when you're nice and when you're mean, and they remember."

"That's stupid," said Simon, his voice cruel and familiar in the dark. Tabitha's joy clattered to the floor, breaking into pieces. "Animals are too dumb to know that stuff."

"Actually, Simon — Tabitha's right," Miss Patterson said. "Crows are highly intelligent creatures. They remember a lot more than other birds — and even some people."

"Like you, Simon," said Jason. A portion of the class laughed, and Miss Patterson scolded them. Simon's silence spoke more harshly to Tabitha than anything he could say. She knew he'd been embarrassed, and even though Jason insulted him, she'd be the one to pay for it.

"Okay, moving on from crows," Miss Patterson continued once the class had settled down, "who can tell me what this bird is?"

As the rest of the class said, "Dodo," Tabitha returned to silence and her doodles. She sketched a picture of Timothy to take her mind off Simon and her classmates. Soon school would be over, and she could see her real friend.

Tabitha clutched the crackers she'd saved from lunch in her pocket. She'd deliberately saved them this time, though it had been difficult. She figured an emptier stomach was worth it if it meant being kind to a friend.

As she rounded the corner, she saw four crows aligned on the fence post. Upon seeing her, three flew up to the tree. One stayed behind. *Squawk!*

"Hello, Timothy," Tabitha replied. She walked up to the fence. Timothy inched back, but stayed on the fence. She was tempted to feed him a cracker from her hand, but she remembered what her mother had said about bites and scratches. Timothy could do either, even by accident. She instead placed the cracker on the fence. Timothy skittered to it quickly, once again downing the cracker in one gulp. *Squawk!*

"You like them, do you?" Tabitha asked, smiling.

"Are you talking to a bird?"

Tabitha jumped at the familiar sound of Simon's cruel voice, a sound she'd thought she'd escaped upon leaving school.

"What are you doing here?" she asked. He didn't live anywhere nearby.

"Is that your crow friend?" he continued, ignoring her. "Hoping he remembers all the nice things you do?"

"I …" She was always at a loss for words around Simon. "I like to feed him, is all. He's kind to me."

Simon sneered. "It would take a dumb animal to be nice to you. Birds of a feather, right?" He laughed at his stupid joke. Tabitha remained quiet, looking at her feet.

Timothy, on the other hand, spoke up. *Squawk, squawk!* He had moved to a post further away, but stayed close enough to flap his wings in Simon's direction, voicing his discontent.

Simon quickly scooped a rock from the ground. "Get out of here, you stupid bird!" Before Tabitha knew it, the rock was airborne, sailing in a straight line towards Timothy.

Fortunately, Timothy was fast — he cleared the post, allowing the rock to sail under his feet. Simon bent down to gather more rocks while Timothy retreated towards the tree.

"No!" Tabitha cried. "You'll hurt him!" She grabbed Simon's arm to try and stop him.

Timothy disappeared into the trees, and Simon wrested his arm from Tabitha's clutch, sending her to the ground. Her glasses fell from her face. She felt her hands scrape as she landed on the rough dirt. Before she could reach them, Simon strode to her glasses and stomped them twice, shattering the lenses.

"See if your crow friend is smart enough to fix this for you," he said, and laughed as he ran off.

Tabitha stayed on the ground until he was out of sight, then sat up and leaned against the fence post. Her palms were bleeding. She picked up the remains of her glasses. Replacing them would be another expense, another burden. She dug a small hole and buried their remains, devising a quick lie to tell her mother about their whereabouts. She'd simply say she lost them. Her mother didn't need to know that someone broke them, someone whose cruelty seemingly followed her wherever she went — even to places where she had found kindness.

She cried quietly. She cried for her glasses, for her mother, for her own pride. Kindness shouldn't be so hard to come by, nor cruelty so easy.

Squawk!

Tabitha looked to her left. Timothy stood on the ground a few feet away. He looked at her quizzically. She wiped her tears. Even if the world wasn't kind, Timothy was — and she could be too. She unearthed the remaining crackers from her pocket — several crushed into pieces — and spread them out over the lower fence post.

"For you and your friends," she said.

Timothy looked at the crackers, then flew to a higher post. He descended again, then dropped a smooth grey stone on the ground. He then flew away.

Tabitha forced a smile, and pocketed the stone. She rose to her feet and started to walk home, preparing to face her mother. She looked behind her, and saw Timothy and four other crows dining on the crackers. Timothy looked up, caught her eye, and flapped his wings.

Tabitha had walked to school in silence the next morning, her heart and eyes in pain. She was back to wearing an old pair of glasses from a year or two ago until she could get new ones. They were too tight and gave her a headache, but it was what she had to deal with.

She hadn't seen Timothy or the other crows. It was just as well — she didn't feel like talking to anyone or anything that day. So it was just her luck that today of all days, Jane rushed to talk to Tabitha as soon as she spotted her in the halls.

"Tabitha!" she yelled. Tabitha tried to ignore her and pretend she hadn't heard, but Jane quickly followed her. "Tabitha, did you hear the news?"

"What news?" Tabitha asked glumly, resigning herself to having to be social.

"About Simon!"

This got Tabitha's attention. She stopped and turned to face Jane, who was wide-eyed and obviously eager to share the news. "No," she said, hoping it was that he'd moved away. "What about him?"

"He was attacked last night," Jane explained, "by wild birds."

Tabitha's own eyes widened. "Wild birds?"

"Yeah!" Jane couldn't hide the hint of excitement behind her tale of horror. "He was throwing rocks at birds last night, and these crows suddenly swooped on him. It was one big one, and then another, until they were all over him."

Tabitha couldn't speak. Jane continued as they walked towards their class. "They were scratching and pecking and everything, and he couldn't get up. They finally left when his mother and brother came outside — they told my mother, that's how I heard, because his brother had to stay with us while his parents took him to the hospital."

"The hospital?" Tabitha asked, and they stopped just outside of their classroom door. "For pecks and scratches?"

"It wasn't just pecks and scratches." Jane looked around her, then dropped her voice to a whisper. "They gouged one of his eyes out."

Tabitha said nothing. Jane took her silence for disbelief, and said, "It's true, I heard his mother say so. She said he'll have a patch for the rest of his life."

The bell rang, and Jane slipped into the classroom. Tabitha stood still a few moments longer. It had to be a crazy rumor. Jane must've misheard Simon's mother.

She walked into the classroom, and noted Simon's empty desk. She sat quietly, thinking about Jane's story. Maybe it could be true after all.

Tabitha stayed away from home after school ended. She leaned against the fence post, deep in thought, watching as the sky turned pink and orange with streaks of blue. She would be home before dark, but she wanted to stay out a little longer.

She stared into the trees and the bramble. There were fewer birds every day, and the evenings grew quieter as winter strolled in. Tabitha felt the wind stinging her cheeks. Soon she wouldn't be able to stay outside for long. Neither would the birds.

She wondered if Timothy and his friends had already left. Perhaps they moved south to get warm. Perhaps they'd fled after what happened to Simon. Surely Simon's mother had called animal control — though Tabitha didn't know how effective they'd be against birds. She hoped animal control hadn't found them, or wouldn't bother trying.

Squawk!

Tabitha did not jump or start. Deep down, she'd known they hadn't left. She'd known they'd come to see her. Deep down, she'd known Jane's story was true.

She turned her head to her left, and saw Timothy alight onto the fence post. She looked at him in silence. She continued watching as Timothy laid what was in his beak on the post.

She knew she should feel sorry for Simon, and chase Timothy and his friends away. Tabitha knew how everyone else would feel had they been there. She knew how Miss Patterson would react, or Jane, or even her mother.

She, however, could not react the way they would. She couldn't ignore the crows, or reject them. She knew that in their own way, the crows had been kind to her. It was their nature — as well as hers.

She gave a small smile. "Thank you, Timothy."

Squawk! Timothy cocked his head, and Tabitha swore it was in salute. After a moment, Timothy quietly fluttered away.

Tabitha watched the trees, listening for any squawks or rustling of wings. Perhaps she'd see them tomorrow. She'd wave to them if they appeared. She'd continue to bring them crackers, and appreciate the gifts they brought her.

She slowly looked away, grateful for their friendship, and closed her hand over a single eye.

I LOVE YOUR WORK

Words meant everything to Ann — especially when they were written by Samuel Miller.

To say that Ann was a bookworm would be an understatement. Even as a little girl, an assortment of authors had passed in and out of her hands — but none had held her quite as tightly as Samuel Miller.

Samuel Miller had floated in and out of Ann's life before she ever read his books. She'd hear his name spoken by her classmates, or see it appear in the credits of a film adaptation of his work. Even though she passed him by on the bookshelves, she could never quite escape him. And even though she'd never read a word he wrote, she had a strange feeling that she should.

When she picked up *First Stop, The Moon*, she felt as if she was visiting a building she'd walked by several times, yet never been inside of before. She finished the story, and liked it, although it hadn't held her much while reading it. As time passed, Samuel Miller's story stayed with her. It wouldn't leave her alone.

She felt a small thrill when she was browsing her library and found a copy of *So Says the River*. She'd first heard the title as she'd heard of Samuel Miller, in passing; and when she saw it sitting primly in the library, its blue cover gleaming against the reds and greys of the surrounding hardbacks, she felt as if it was being offered to her. She grabbed it immediately.

So Says the River was a much different experience from *First Stop, the Moon*. Starting with the first page, Ann felt under a spell. Simple words formed elegant sentences, and she found herself immersed in the depths of Samuel Miller's prose. Her heart ached for the story. She felt it in parts of her brain she'd never given to stories before. She'd paused after the final page, staring at the book as if closing it would make it disappear. She'd placed her fingers on the page, touching the final sentences.

She'd vowed, then and there, to read whatever words he wrote. She read more of his books, loving some, feeling indifferent towards others. Even her least favorite stories found their way into her heart. She also followed him on social media and read interviews here and there, combing through the words that hadn't been collected in stories. Samuel Miller's words wrapped themselves around her like a security blanket. He connected with her — but only through the printed page.

In all her years of knowing Samuel Miller, she had never had the chance to meet him. There were opportunities, of course. He often came through her area on book tours, or announced festival appearances, or attended the occasional panel at a convention. But whenever there was a chance to meet him, it seemed like fate intervened to ensure that Ann wouldn't be able to do so. On his last book tour, she had been in New York City the same day he was in town. The local book festival he was to appear at sold out before she had a chance to buy tickets. It seemed to Ann that no matter what, something kept her from meeting Samuel Miller.

So, in her senior year of college, when Ann saw that he was scheduled to do a signing at her local bookstore, she became determined to not let the opportunity pass. She noted the date, and quickly scribbled the signing onto her calendar. She already had a copy of the book he was promoting, *A Life in Cinema Cells*, and carefully chose other books of his to bring.

Two days before the signing, Ann was browsing Twitter, and saw Samuel Miller post about his appearance: "Friends: don't forget, I'll be at the Olive Branch Bookstore on Thursday, 9 PM to close, signing my new book." Ann smiled, thinking, *I'll be there too.* Her thoughts coursed through her fingertips, and she typed to him in response, "I'll be there. Looking forward to meeting you! I love your work." She'd written him before, and though she knew her words were drowned in the sea of replies he received, she sent them to him all the same, hoping their existence was enough to tell him she was there.

An hour later, as she sat studying for an exam, her phone buzzed. She looked down and, to her delight, saw Samuel Miller's name appear on her phone. He had responded to her tweet: "Thank you Ann. I look forward to meeting you too."

Thank you Ann. His tweet pulsed through her fingertips with the same intensity as his books. He'd seen her words. He'd read them. He'd thanked her for them.

Yes, he was just being polite. No, she wasn't expecting a friendship to blossom between them. His words meant so much to her, though, that she simply wanted him to know that, to know how much his words mattered in her life. He knew, and told her so. And tomorrow, she would be able to tell him in person — or so she hoped.

The next morning, Ann was browsing her social networks and saw news from The Olive Branch — there had been a small fire overnight. There wasn't significant damage, but the store would be closed while they assessed the situation.

Ann was crestfallen. A fire? Surely the universe had it out for her. She was glad that no one had been hurt and that the bookstore — one of her favorite places, whether or not Samuel Miller was in it — remained standing. Yet she couldn't help feeling perturbed at what looked to be yet another lost opportunity to meet him.

Ann tried to focus on other things, but her exam notes were gibberish in her current state of mind. She spent the day in a stressed blur, and only slept fitfully that night. She checked The Olive Branch's page as soon as she woke up, and was delighted to see an update: "We're open! Stop by and say hello. And even better news — Samuel Miller will still be able to attend his scheduled signing. Doors open at 9, so be sure to come by!"

Ann did a small dance on her bed. The store wasn't closed, and Samuel Miller was still coming! Maybe, just maybe, today would be her day. She spent the day's remaining hours in orbit, only coming down from her dream state to study for tomorrow's exam. She sped through dinner, spent some time getting dressed, gathered her books for Samuel Miller to sign, and walked quickly to the bus stop. She'd be there right at nine, maybe a little bit after, but still on time to meet him.

Time passed, but her expected bus didn't arrive. She checked the bus schedule on the stop post, and saw that not one, but two buses should've arrived by now. Where were they?

She pulled up the bus information on her phone, and groaned. The bus on this route had been cancelled. Maintenance. *Great*, she thought, *just great. Couldn't they have put up a sign at the damn stop?*

Ann still had time. She pulled up Uber and saw that cars were available. Within five minutes, a driver pulled up and asked if she was Ann.

"Yes, I am," she said as she climbed in. *Nice try, universe.*

She should've known better. They were rolling along the highway, Ann flipping through *A Life in Cinema Cells*, when she felt the car come to an abrupt stop. "What's going on?" she asked.

"Traffic," the driver answered, not proving to be very helpful.

It's fine, she thought. *Highways have traffic. We'll be moving.*

Time went by, and the traffic didn't ebb. Ann read a whole chapter of her book before she realized they'd barely moved. She arched her neck to look ahead. "What's going on?"

"It looks like there was an accident," the driver said, scrolling through his own phone. "We'll be moving soon, but they're trying to direct everyone around it."

Are you fucking kidding me? Ann looked around her. They were surrounded by cars, trees, and stretches of highway — no exit ramps nearby. *Fuck!*

She slammed her head against the backseat, trying to breathe easier. Worrying wouldn't make the traffic magically go away. She tried reading some more, hoping to take her mind off things; though her heart thumped whenever they moved, and sank when they'd stop a few moments later.

"Are you in a hurry?" the driver asked.

"I'm trying to get to a signing," Ann replied, checking her phone. It was past 9 o'clock. Samuel Miller was already there, probably with a huge line of people. She looked out the window, and wondered if she stared hard enough, the other cars would get going out of fear.

"Well, once I see an exit, I'll get off the highway," the driver offered. "We can get to the bookstore another way."

Ann smiled weakly. He was trying. "Thanks." She picked her book back up, not wanting to talk, and not wanting to focus on her miserable luck.

Slowly but surely, the car began to move more than a few seconds at a time. It was when they picked up speed that Ann dared to look up. They were leaving the highway. The road was clear! Maybe she'd make it after all.

"Okay," the driver said, "I think there's a back way along here, only a couple miles away —"

He'd barely spoken the words when a deer leapt in front of the car. Ann screamed and the driver swerved, barely missing the deer as its hooves glided gracefully over the car. The car was less graceful, swerving and jerking before skidding to a stop. They were okay, but Ann's heart sank as she heard a loud pop under the car.

"Dammit!" the driver yelled as he bolted out of the car. Ann stared blankly ahead of her, wondering what else would keep her away from Samuel Miller.

The driver stood up after a few minutes and tapped her window. She opened the door, and he confirmed what she feared: "It's a flat tire. I don't have a spare either."

Great, just great. She closed her eyes.

"I can cancel the trip, give you a refund …"

None of those offers would make up for missing Samuel Miller. She sighed, and put her head in her hands.

"I'm really sorry."

She looked back up, and tried to keep her face calm. It wasn't his fault that everything around her was trying their absolute hardest to keep her from meeting Samuel Miller. "It's okay," she said. "I'm just in a hurry to get somewhere."

"Well, I can't get you there until I call someone to help."

"I know," Ann said, getting out of the car. "Thank you, though, for trying. I'm sorry about your car."

They exchanged goodbyes, and Ann left the driver to curse over his rotten luck. It was okay, she was only a couple miles away. She could get another car. She pulled out her phone as she walked down the street, ready to make the call, and saw with a sinking heart that her battery was dead.

Okay. No car whatsoever. She looked up the road. She recognized this street. It ended at The Olive Branch. The driver had said they were a couple miles away.

When she'd last checked her phone, she'd had a little under an hour before close.

She set her jaw. "I'm coming, Sam."

She strode on the sidewalk as fast as she could. It was dark, and growing cool. She saw the moon disappear, and wondered what would happen next. Would a tornado blow through? Would more deer stampede across her path? Would a madman jump out of the woods and kidnap her?

When it happened, it was something less sinister, but no less aggravating. She tripped on a raised piece of sidewalk, and skidded across the ground when she landed on it. She turned herself over, examining her scraped palms and scuffed jeans.

"Come on!" she shouted at the trees, having no one else to blame. "What's your fucking problem? Can't you just let me get to the store?" She hung her head, and her eyes welled up. "I just want to meet him. Why is it so hard?"

She looked at her fallen bag. The books hadn't scattered, thankfully, but *So Says the River* peeked out from the top. She blinked back her tears before they could fall, and delicately picked up the book. It felt warm in her hands. Comforting. She opened the book to Chapter One and traced her fingers over the words, taking in the power they had over her.

"I will meet him," she said. "I don't care what the universe thinks."

She hoisted herself up, wincing, but not unable to stand. Hoisting her bag over her shoulder, she continued on, barely looking at anything but what was ahead. She ignored the gusts of wind that blew against her, only blinking against a few drops of rain that started to fall. She would not be stopped. The universe seemed to take notice, as the rain remained meek.

At last, she saw a shopping center in front of her, with The Olive Branch gleaming in front. Ann sighed, smiling as she took it in. She trotted to the store, heart thumping. To her relief, the lights were still on, and the door opened. She was here — and so was he. This was actually happening.

She saw a lone sign with an arrow pointing up that proclaimed: "Come upstairs if you want to meet Samuel Miller." *You don't even know the half of it*, she thought with a small smile as she bounded up the stairs. They were closing soon, but they weren't closed, not yet.

She stopped at the top of the stairs, and her eyes widened. There he was. Samuel Miller.

She took him in, and how he towered over both an empty table and the bookstore manager who spoke to him. His dark brown hair rested neatly behind his ears, his deep green eyes shined as he spoke, and his long white fingers placed a brown notebook in a black messenger bag.

Her eyes quickly widened in dismay. Samuel Miller was leaving.

"Wait!"

The word escaped her lips before she'd paused to think how the exclamation, and her disheveled look from the walk and the fall, might make her look crazy. The manager and Samuel Miller both paused, looking up at her in shock.

"I'm here for the signing. I know I'm a bit late, but …"

"I'm sorry," the manager said, "we're closing up shop. The signing's done."

Ann's heart sank, but she continued. She had nothing to lose. "Please, Jim," she said, stealing a look at his nametag and keeping her tone steady.

She shifted her eyes to Samuel Miller, who looked at her quizzically. "I've wanted to meet you for so long. I love your work."

His eyes fixed steadily on hers. He asked softly, "Are you Ann?"

Her heart soared. He remembered her. "Yes!" she said, beaming. "I'm Ann Monroe, and I love your stories. Just five minutes, please."

"Miss Monroe …" Jim began, but Samuel Miller raised a hand to silence him. "It's all right," he said. "Just one more. I can stay."

Jim paused, nodded, and quietly walked past her. Ann strode to the table where Samuel Miller had taken his seat. The brown notebook was back on the table, alongside two pens.

"Thank you so much," Ann breathed, lifting her books from her bag. "It's such an honor to finally meet you. I've wanted to for so long."

"Not a problem," Samuel Miller replied, smiling at her before turning his gaze to the books she lay in front of him. "I always have time for fans."

He began to sign, and Ann continued as collectedly as she could, "You're my favorite writer. I must've read *So Says the River* —" which Samuel Miller was now signing — "three times at least. It's wonderful."

"Thank you," he said, moving to *A Life in Cinema Cells*. Ann didn't know what to say next, but hated the silence. She chuckled softly. "I almost can't believe I'm meeting you. I always seem to miss you. Even tonight, I almost missed you again." He smiled. With a wider grin, she added, "It's almost like something out there was determined to keep me away from you."

"Something probably was," Samuel Miller said softly, finishing his signature.

Ann wasn't sure she'd heard him correctly. Her brow furrowed. "I'm sorry?"

"Something probably was," he repeated, "because it knew what would happen if we met."

She sat in silence. What did he mean by that? He closed the book and looked up at her, smiling; and her confusion vanished. He kept her gaze and asked, "Would you like to see what I'm working on?"

Ann's heart soared. "Yes!" she exclaimed, then flushed at losing her cool. "Yes," she repeated, softer now. He chuckled politely. "Wow, thank you."

Samuel Miller dragged the brown leather notebook closer to them, moving it towards Ann. She held her hand over it. She could almost feel it pulling her to open it. Should she?

"Go ahead," he said. "Take a look."

She hesitated a moment more, then opened it carefully. She saw notes on the pages, an occasional doodle, but mostly scratched-out ideas and stray sentences in need of a home. Even detached from a story, without context and characters, his words were beautiful. She couldn't wait to see the finished product.

"It's in pieces now," he said. "It just needs one more bit, and then it'll be ready."

"Like what?" she asked absently, turning the pages. She could even get lost in his notes. Outside she heard a sudden gust of wind. It almost sounded like a sigh.

"Like you."

This got her attention. She looked up at him.

His face stayed neutral, but his eyes blazed. Ann felt uneasy, yet unable to move or let go of the page.

"I need you, Ann."

Her body grew cold. "I don't understand," she said.

"You always hear writers say they couldn't do what they do without their fans." He calmly lifted his other pen. "They mean it, in their own way, but it's still just a figure of speech." His eyes locked onto hers. "Not for me."

He clasped her wrist, and she barely jumped, so intense was his stare. "I couldn't do what I do without my fans," he continued, "because then what I do wouldn't exist. I need them, Ann. I need you." He smiled warmly, dangerously; her heart began to race. "And at last, I have you."

Her trance was broken by a searing pain across her palm. She looked down and saw his pen hovering above her hand. It took a second longer to realize he wasn't holding a pen, but a knife. Her hand was bleeding onto the page.

Her mouth dropped open, but she only managed to breathe quickly. Screaming was seemingly out of her reach. Samuel Miller's grip was strong, and she watched as her blood dripped on his words. He turned her arm and pressed her palm onto the notebook. The page seared her quickly, a burn that faded into a stronger version of the sensation she felt when she'd read his books, when she'd touched his words.

Next to her hand, the notes and scribbles began to move. They swam in her blood, swirling and twisting as they changed from notes into sentences, scribbles into prose. They surfaced anew as the words which sustained her for years. As they completed themselves, she looked back at her hand and saw it was gone. She was wrist-deep in the notebook, and felt herself being pulled further and further in. Pages flipped and the sensation intensified as each paragraph completed itself. Everything around her was fading quickly. She finally managed a scream. At last the notebook snapped shut, and Samuel Miller held it in his hands.

"Thank you, Ann." He packed his pens and notebook, and stood up to depart.

Jim came back upstairs, his voice entering a few moments before him. "Okay Miss Monroe, Mr. Miller," he called. "It's past close, we really have to —"

Jim stopped, looking at the empty table. Samuel Miller finished buttoning his coat, looking at Jim casually. Jim stood, looking confused. "Where'd she go?" he asked. "I didn't see her leave."

"Who?" Samuel Miller replied, looking at Jim calmly. "I was just packing up."

Jim stood still, wondering. His brow lost its furrow. "Oh," he said at last. "Right. The last guy left a while ago. That's right."

Samuel Miller smiled. Of course that was right. He was the author. He controlled the story.

"Well, thank you for coming, Mr. Miller," Jim continued. "Your driver's out front."

"Thank you," Samuel Miller replied. He swept past Jim and exited the store. He entered the waiting car, and pulled out his notebook as he rode to his hotel, writing one final piece: *Ann went missing, but nobody looked for her.*

I NEVER KNEW
YOUR NAME

Cities are filled with familiar strangers. That is how I knew you. I saw you every day, but I never knew your name.

There are enough people in the city to sift through them anonymously, but also enough doing the same thing as you, going the same way you're going, that you get to know them in everything but name.

I saw you each day on my way to work, as I see many. We surely all recognize each other, but only you made eye contact with me. Only you smiled and said, "Good morning, ma'am."

And though I normally prefer familiar strangers to keep their distance, I too smiled at you. I too waved at you. I too said, "Good morning."

That was the start, and end, of our friendship. We'd pass each other each day, smile, wave, and say "Good morning." No more, no less.

I wondered, as the days and our greetings grew in number, what connected us apart from all the others. I'd never seen you anywhere but that sidewalk. No one else spoke to you, and you spoke to no one else.

Perhaps you didn't want them to see you. Perhaps I saw you by accident. I saw you in the morning on my way to work, then promptly forgot you.

I only thought of my morning paper, with its distraught headlines: war, famine, a local child missing. There were wars every day, hungry people everywhere, many children who had disappeared. I turned the page and read the comics.

I continued to see you. We would say good morning. You'd walk by others in silence. I would read my paper.

Continued war, continued famine, two more local children gone missing. Wars continued, famine continued, but children didn't disappear from my neighborhood each day. I read the comics, but thought of the three local children who were gone. Where did they go?

As we passed each other, I'd wonder things about you. Where were you from? Why were you walking opposite the workflow? Did you work at night? I began to think of you even when we didn't share a sidewalk. I'd seen you so often, you were almost my friend. One whose name I didn't know.

Another child missing — and the other three had yet to be found. I couldn't read the comics.

No one else even waved to you, much less spoke to you. Could they see you? Were you a ghost? A spirit? A floating friend to greet me hello each morning?

Three more children missing. One of the first to go missing had been found by a riverbank. There were pictures in the paper. She looked … empty, like the life had been vacuumed from her, like her soul had been drained. People wondered what mysterious stranger would take them away.

Like many familiar strangers, you began to flicker out of my routine. Days would go by where I wouldn't see you, and I thought you'd found a new job, or moved away. But then you'd reappear. We'd smile, and wave, and say, "Good morning." You never said anything more. Maybe you didn't want to tell me more.

More children were found. They all looked like the drained girl. A few more disappeared, but now the papers said they found a pattern, a path to lead them to the attacker. Fewer children went missing. I saw you less and less.

Soon no children went missing. The news moved on to celebrities and politicians.

Soon you were gone forever. And I never knew your name.

ALL THE PIECES COMING TOGETHER

The branches whip in the wind as the sky bruises and bleeds into night. A lone bird chirps, desperately seeking a mate, but the only call back is the rustle of pine needles that cling to their branches. There is not a human soul for miles.

It's the perfect place to hide a body. The trouble is, there isn't anybody to hide.

I'm a serial killer — or at least, I would be if there were anyone around to kill. I picked an amazing spot to begin my life of murderous solitude. I soon realized it was a little too solitary, though, so my career has largely been dicking around online (when I can get a connection) and watching movies.

I've had some practice, of course. I began where we almost all begin: helpless animals. They were easy to start with because many people didn't think twice about them. "Oh, don't mind him, he's just a boy

— boys sometimes hurt animals." Normal boys sometimes squash bugs or kick the family pet. A normal boy doesn't dismember dogs and bury each piece in a different part of the woods that, if unearthed, would spell their name in binary code.

It's a good thing I started with animals, because that's all I've got out here. I even tried to get as creative as I would with a person. Unfortunately, the deer just can't pick up on the patterns. I worked really hard to shape their limbs into that peace sign, and what did they do? Nothing. Ungrateful bastards.

Further, there are too many deer for their absence to make much difference. People are limited, which makes their disposal all the more rewarding. Their disappearance leads to a crisis, which leads to a puzzle, one that I've created and know they'll never solve. People are limited. People are missed.

I miss them.

I want to be near them again. We all want closeness and companionship. Some of us just gain that by burying people in the floorboards. The floorboards of my lonely cabin, in these lonely woods, where no one can find them — and where I can't find anyone.

I need to get out of the woods and find some people.

First, I need to find a place to go.

Fortunately, my Internet is working, perhaps suggesting that tonight is my night. I look at what's around here. Not much of anything, naturally. There are schools further out, but it's late and most students will have walked home alone by now. There are churches, but I don't trust anyone in church on a Tuesday.

Ah, here we go — a bar, called The Best Shot. Fitting, as it's my best chance at finding someone tonight. It's about an hour away, though I could probably speed most of the way without fail. There aren't any cops out here either.

I quickly make myself presentable. I shave the scant beard I've grown and run a comb through my short brown hair. Before moving here, I was a man who'd charmed quite a few panties into my palm. I was ready to turn that charm back on, albeit for a much different purpose.

I hop in my piece-of-shit car and drive down the highway. It's a pretty night — lots of stars, a cool breeze. It is insanely dark. It's the kind that can almost make you feel enclosed by its opacity. My first couple nights sleeping out here, I almost had panic attacks. I couldn't see my own hands in front of my face. What if I could never see again? What if darkness was all I had left? At least in death, you're unaware of the darkness surrounding you. It's a courtesy I hope to extend to others.

The road drags on endlessly, even as I speed. Fortunately no deer are slowing me down. Maybe my artwork is working well enough to deter them from running in front of my car.

Slowly the darkness opens into streetlamps and a Wal-Mart. It's always the first sign of civilization when you leave the middle of nowhere. The lone Wal-Mart gives way to occasional gas stations, ones so isolated that I'm sure you could see Jason Voorhees pumping gas and not think twice. The gas stations become strip malls and the strip malls become chain restaurants.

Finally, tucked between some pine trees just past a Lowes, I see it — The Best Shot. I'm relieved to see some cars parked out front. I'd worried slightly that even if there were people around, they'd be choosing to smoke meth in the privacy of their own garden sheds instead of getting drunk in a bar.

I walk inside, and it looks like every stereotype of a podunk bar you'd come to expect: one of the nation's last surviving jukeboxes, an assortment of old men and hard women, and a bartender who probably got a few of her tats in prison. The scent of vodka and beer hangs in the air, and it looks like the kind of place that would've smelled of cigarettes if it weren't against the law to smoke inside. This is one law I'm thankful for. An asthma attack is the last thing I need when scouting potential victims.

I move towards the bar, some money in my pocket. I came prepared for a couple of beers — enough to seem loose (and loosen up) while staying sober enough to drive someone back to the middle of nowhere. I'm not going to be driven home by someone and then kill them in their own house. I'm perfectly able to host a murder, thank you.

I take a seat, and the bartender comes over with a look on her face that tells me she'd rather be anywhere than here. "What'll it be, hon," she says as a statement, not a question. Age and — from the sound of it — smoking since kindergarten have not been kind to her.

"Just a Bud, please." Do people still drink Bud? I keep reading about craft beer online. I doubt this place even knows what craft beer is.

She wordlessly pours my Bud, one of two tap handles (confirming my craft beer suspicions), and places it in front of me.

"Keeping it simple, huh?"

I stop mid-sip and look in the direction of the voice. I see a woman I hadn't noticed previously. She's suspiciously hot in these surroundings. Auburn hair in a ponytail, rimless glasses, tits peeking out over a pink bustier. She's drinking what looks like a whiskey sour, dunking the maraschino cherry up and down in the ice. The effect causes a ripple in her breasts, one I try very hard not to stare at.

"Simple?" I ask. Well, stammer. I am a cool and collected killer, but I am also a warm-blooded man, one who hasn't even seen a woman in a very long time.

"'Just a Bud, please.'" Her imitation man voice makes her sound even sexier. Jesus, I hadn't accounted for being turned on. "You're just going to ask for that? You're not going to see what else they have to offer?"

I sip my beer to try and quell my ever-growing boner, and say calmly, coolly, "Well, forgive me for assuming that this place doesn't have much creativity to offer."

She has a small and wispy laugh that disappears like a puff of smoke. Her eyes reconnect with mine, and she says, "Sometimes all you have to do is ask." Her eyes don't leave mine as she slowly bites one of the cherries and sucks it off the stem.

That's it. Killing is 50/50, but I'm definitely fucking tonight.

I scooch one barstool over so that I'm next to her. She doesn't move, much to my delight, and we start the small talk that precludes fucking. I tell her my name, that I work in lumber and live out near the woods. It's lonely, but it pays the bills. I'm hopeful that sympathy works in my sexual favor — as does buying the next round, which I do at this point.

Her name is Candace, and she's a nurse. She's off tonight, and she figured she'd stop in for a drink or two, have a little fun, maybe find a little trouble. Our knees have moved toward each other at this point, so she has no problem dropping her finger on my wrist when she says this.

I stare at her finger with its perfect pink tip. I imagine it disconnected from her bangled wrist, floating over my own. Each piece of her starts to detach from itself, floating in various places in my mind. The human body is nothing but fragments, held together by sinew and bone; and I can take it apart, piece-by-piece. I can reassemble as I wish, or scatter the pieces to points of no return. It's a control I crave, one that, combined with the sexual longing an average person would be feeling right now, begins to consume me. I can feel my dick stiffening against my pants, my pulse raising rapidly.

It's the pulse that Candace notices first. She places more fingers on my wrist, turning it over. I let her. Giving her some control now will make it easier to completely master her later. I already imagine her hands on my face, her legs on my bed, her breasts on my mantle. I can't wait any longer.

"All I have to do is ask, right?"

She returns her gaze to me, and gives me a sly smile. "Depends on the question."

I take a final gulp of beer. "Do you want to get out of here?"

Everything is going according to plan. Well, it will once we stop making out.

We haven't even left the parking lot of The Best Shot. One minute I'm all set to drive her to the cabin, and then she brushed my hair before I could open the passenger-side door, and I couldn't help myself and we started kissing against the car. No, kissing's too demure a way to describe it. The only thing keeping us from getting arrested is the fact that we have our clothes on.

I'm not one of those killers who's afraid of sex or women, or can only do it on top of a corpse or in a bathtub full of someone's blood or something. I love sex. Another disadvantage of my chosen locale. I really didn't think that one through. And now, I risk letting my hormones get the better of me and precluding Candace from reaching her final destination.

"We've gotta get to my place," I manage to croak out. She continues kissing my neck while I speak, and I can feel her breasts brushing against my shoulder.

"Okay," is all she manages to say. I've moved to her shoulder, and we move back to each other's mouths. I run my hands up and down her sides and she grabs my ass, grinding against me. Surely she can feel my erection. I contemplate just doing it on the hood of the car.

"The sooner we get home," I say, pulling myself away again, "the sooner we can do this right."

This stops us both. She turns back to face the car, and I open the door before I have a chance to change my mind and start taking her from behind. She's barely in before I slam the door shut, rush to the driver's side, and peel out of the parking lot, heading home for an evening of sex and murder. My heart — not to mention my prick — can barely stand it.

The road is even emptier than when I made my way out here earlier. Candace rolls down the window and lets her fingers float in the breeze, arching her back ever-so-slightly against the seat and letting out a delicate moan of pleasure. She's pleasing herself, playing with me, or maybe a little of both. I try to keep my eyes ahead of me. The last thing I want is a car wreck to rob me of this kill.

"You really do live far away," she says after we've been driving for some time, when the strip malls have become the lone Wal-Mart but have not yet become trees again.

"I like to be near the source of my work," I say. This in itself isn't necessarily a lie.

"I kind of like it," she replies. "Seems peaceful."

I sigh, thinking of how long it's been since I've had sex, and of all of the dead deer. "Sometimes it's too peaceful."

I feel her hand slink down onto my leg, and hear her seatbelt unbuckle. She moves closer to me, and I pray she isn't contemplating road head — it would be amazing, but I really need to be able to drive.

Her head stays above my pants, though, and rests on my shoulder. She whispers, "It won't be tonight." And then she bites my ear.

I speed up substantially. We have to get home.

In my chosen line of work, it helps to be handsome. Drawing people in is part of the battle. People have to trust you if you're going to successfully kill them. A great way to get people to trust you is to get them to want to fuck you. And a great way to get them to want to fuck you is to be handsome. Which, fortunately, I am. At least that's what I tell myself. Otherwise, the fact that my potential victim has gone from straddling a barstool to straddling my lap in roughly three hours just seems a little too easy.

We've made it to the house — well, to my driveway. We have yet to get out of the car. As soon as I put the car in park, we started making out again. Candace's jacket is in the backseat, but otherwise, we stay clothed. This hasn't stopped me from rubbing her through her panties, or her from grinding on my cock.

"Let's go inside," she finally breathes. I almost don't hear her, as I'm focused entirely on her body. Seduction was a tactic I had in mind, but this is bordering on madness. I cannot stop touching her, nor her me. I try to cool myself off by thinking of the after party, of carving her up and spreading the pieces, but this only makes it worse. It gives me a secret, one she'll never know until it's too late. And here she is, giving herself to me. It's too delicious to bear.

And giving herself she is — in full. We make it into the house, finally, but only to the couch. She drops her giant purse on the floor, a loud thwack echoing across the floorboards as she quickly sheds pieces of clothing: glasses, jewelry, skirt. My shirt and belt follow suit, until I'm down to my briefs and she's annoyingly clad in her underwear and bustier.

I grab at her top and she takes my hands, showing the first sign of resistance all night. She pushes my hands away, holding them firmly on the couch.

"What are you …" I start to say, praying she isn't stopping things here. I also start to contemplate a much sooner death for her than I anticipated.

But she interrupts me, placing one hand over my lips. I forget my frustration and start biting her thumb. She takes it back and slowly unfastens her bustier from the back. It's the slowest thing she's done all night, and it's worth it.

The moment her breasts spill into view, things become an immediate blur. I'm aware of launching myself into them, kissing and biting with abandon while she holds my head close and groans with pleasure. Soon we're standing up, because a couch is a fine place for fucking, but not nearly as good as a bed. Hell, it's not even as good as a kitchen table, where we make a pit stop so I can pull down her panties and start eating her out.

I am aware, as we stand back up and continue on to the bedroom, that my plans have gone somewhat off course. I'd forgotten how hard it is to stay focused when a hot naked woman is present. But for the time being, as we roll around over my old comforter, I don't care. Her time will come. For now I'll happily kiss and bite various places on her skin, groan while she scratches my back, and thrust my cock inside of her from various positions.

I could fuck her all night and probably most of the next, but I'm only able to come so much. I lay next to her, regrettably spent, as she is still able to cuddle on me and nibble my earlobe. Women will never know how lucky they are to be able to keep going after they come. Hell, at least with Candace, coming seems to make her want more.

She slows when she sees that, for me at least, the fucking is finished. "Where's your bathroom?" she asks. I merely point, still out of breath. I pray this is the only indication I might have given her of how long it's been since I've had sex. I watch her as she walks, naked, to the living room to grab her purse and then shuts herself in the bathroom. I hear her loudly pee.

Okay, maybe now I can begin to focus. What next? I recall my various hiding places for assorted weapons and drugs. None of them are immediately under the bed. I could go looking for them while she's in the bathroom. Then I hear her flush, and abandon that idea. The door stays closed, and I hear her rummaging through her purse, brushing her hair. Time is slipping away.

Stay the night — she'll probably stay the night. I did drive her here, after all. I'm her ride home. *In more ways than one.* I smile, and feel myself stiffen again. She'll fall asleep, breathing lightly next to me, and then …

I'm broken from my glimpse in the future by the sound of the bathroom door opening. I look forward and she's back — hair brushed, fresh coat of lipstick, still naked. Her purse is in her hand. Her eyes fall on my newly-awakened cock and she smiles. "Not completely spent, huh?" she says, moving towards me.

I don't want to make her promises I can't keep, but it's hard to speak as she drops her purse on the bedside table and straddles over me. "I — I guess not …" I manage to say, before I'm silenced by her mouth.

Okay, no falling asleep yet. I'll deal. I run my hands over her ass, kissing her, keeping it slow. She grinds on top of me while her hands run all over my body. Well, her hand. Where's her other hand?

She pulls away, and I realize three things — both my legs and one arm are pinned under her surprisingly-strong legs, one hand is pinning my free arm down, and her other hand is pressing a rag into my face. It smells off. Oh fuck, oh fuck, OH FU —

Thankfully I wake up. I'm still naked and still in bed. Now I'm tightly secured to the bedposts by my wrists and ankles. The room gradually comes into focus. I don't see Candace. Where did she go?

I can't believe this. I knew it was too easy. I never should have let her take control like that. God, letting her get on top? Yes, hindsight is 20/20. But you need to be more aware. Victims don't fall into your lap, and Candace isn't a victim, not by a long shot.

Candace isn't even here. Where the fuck is she? Did she just decide to tie me up and peace out? Maybe she took the car. Well, I won't exactly miss it. But these binds are pretty strong — they'll take hours to get out of if I'm here alone.

I hear her footsteps, dashing that theory aside. Then what? I don't suppose she's secretly into BDSM and this is just a precursor to more sex.

My vision is almost completely focused, and restores itself just in time to see her walk into the room. She's no longer naked, but wearing purple nursing scrubs, just unfastened enough to show her cleavage.

Where did she get those from? I notice her purse in her gloved hands. It's huge — probably big enough for the scrubs. And the rag. What else?

"Oh good," she says, stopping next to the bed. She rubs her hand through my hair. What had been a major turn-on now sends a sickening chill down my neck. My toes curl and my heart rate quickens. "You're awake."

"What the fuck is going on?" I ask. She gets on top of me again. It's amazing how that suddenly feels old and unwelcome. "What the fuck did you do to me?"

"Just put you to sleep for a little bit," she replies, tracing her fingers over my chest.

"Put me to sleep?" I snort in disgust. "You knocked me out, you fucking bitch. Why did you tie me up?" I give her a coy look, one final bit of hope. "If you were into this, you could've just asked."

She laughs. It's a little sexy, but mostly ugly. I do the worst thing any potential serial killer could do: I get scared. I don't like the way she's touching me, especially as her fingers near my throat. I start panicking, thinking she must know who I am, what I am, and plans to stop it. To stop me.

"Look," I say, just wanting my own freedom at this point. "Whatever you think, it's … just let me go. I'll drive you back, and we can go our separate ways. I won't hurt you, I promise, I —"

A flash of genuine confusion crosses her face before it disappears and settles into smug control. "Hurt me?" She leers. "You can't."

"And I won't," I continue. "I don't know what you thought, why you wanted to tie me up, what you know or think or figured out …" Her face stays stoic, though I can see her thoughts racing. "But whatever it is, I won't do it. Not now."

"Do what?" she asks.

I mentally kick myself for panicking. I sigh, resigning myself to just telling the truth. "I won't … you know, kill you."

She stares at me blankly for a few long moments. Then she cocks her head, keeping eye contact with me as she straightens her posture. Her hands leave my chest.

"I didn't tie you up because I thought you were going to kill me," she says at last. I quietly sigh, and simultaneously feel my heart sink.

I notice that one hand is reaching into her purse. My pulse races as she withdraws a single, sharp scalpel.

"I tied you up," she says, looking me dead in the eyes, "because I'm going to kill you."

You've got to be shitting me.

I stare at her. I'm not even scared. I'm fucking pissed. "You're fucking kidding me, right?"

I can tell she was expecting a different reaction. She can't hide the flicker of disappointment that runs across her eyes. "No," she says, trying to scare me — and failing. "I'm not kidding. I'm going to kill you."

I roll my eyes so far back that she almost won't need to bother gouging them out if she wants to. I finally leave this fucking cabin, finally go scouting for victims, finally find one, and it turns out that she was also scouting. Just fucking great. I knew it was too easy.

"Un-fucking-believable." I laugh, which I'm sure only confuses her more. "So this whole time, you were luring me?"

"Yes." She stays still, but her stoic expression is wavering.

"And you picked me out, and came home with me, and intended to kill me this entire time?"

"Yes."

"So the talking, the flirting, the sex ... that was all one big orchestration to kill me?"

"The first two, yes." She's lowered the scalpel by now, but it still rests in her hand and against my hip. "I didn't originally plan the sex, but —"

"You didn't?!" I jerk back up, careful not to jar the scalpel too much. I feel it just barely poke into my hip, and still wince. Christ it's sharp. "You decided to kill me, then changed your mind and decided to fuck me first?" The irony of my anger is not lost on me, but I'm too furious and, frankly, too embarrassed to care.

"Well, why not? It's been awhile since I've gotten laid, and well ..." She shrugs and smiles a bit. "I wanted to fuck you. You're pretty hot."

See, what did I tell you? It pays to be handsome. Well, except for right now.

Her voice brings me back into focus. "You said you wouldn't kill me now." She presses her hand closer to my hip, and I wince involuntarily, despite the blade not pushing further. "What did you mean by that?"

I'm too focused on the scalpel to answer her right away. It's also too humiliating. I not only have to admit I had almost the exact same reasoning as she did — even down to taking a side trip to have sex first — but I in turn have to admit that I failed at it. She's won,

I've lost. And I've lost because of my own stupidity. I deserve to die.

"What did you mean by that?" she asks again, pointing the blade against my side.

I bring my thoughts back to her — well, her scalpel. I'm going to die, but I don't want to sooner than I have to.

"I meant what you probably think," I say, looking her cold in the face. I'm doomed. I'm already tied up. I have nothing left, and nothing to hide. I set my jaw, lift my head up a bit. "I brought you here to kill you."

She doesn't change her expression, and I continue. "Yes, you picked me before I picked you. I picked you after I saw you. I picked you because you were coming onto me, because I wanted you and figured I could get some action before killing you. And yeah, I put it off because I wanted to get laid. I think you're hot too.

"So yes, Candace, I had every intention of murdering you tonight. I mean, Jesus, look around you." I wave my head around the span of the cabin. "Why the fuck do you think I live out here in this godforsaken cabin? It makes it easier to hide people when they're dead!"

"Yeah, I noticed that," she says, interrupting me. "I couldn't believe my luck when you said you lived out in the woods. This place looked like a dream come true when you pulled into the driveway. It's the perfect place to hide you afterward."

See? It's the perfect place to hide the bodies. I'm so good at planning murders, I perfectly planned my own.

"So I know why you're here, and what you're doing," I continue. "Because it's what I was going to do to you. We're exactly the same."

"Not exactly," she says, coldness entering her voice once more. She delicately runs the scalpel over my chest. "We were both going to fuck the other one over. But the difference?"

A sudden rush of nausea runs over me, as I guess what's going to happen next: she's going to try and be clever. I swear to God, if she says she came first …

She leans next to my ear. "I came first."

I should've killed her sooner.

***

"Why?"

She ceases making a long, shallow cut up my chest — the third such cut she's made — and looks up at me, glaring. Her expression matches the cuts she's already made over my skin. Just my luck that I not only pick up a killer, but one who likes to draw out the pain.

"Why what?" she asks, thankfully pausing for a moment. "Why you? Why now?"

"No," I say, breathing deeply and trying to not notice the growing pool of blood on the sheets. She'll have a hell of a time cleaning them up. I hope pieces of me get all over her. Good luck covering your tracks, you cunt. "Why killing?"

She laughs. "My motive? You want me to go all James Bond villain on you?"

"Come on, I'm about to die. If you're not going to kill me straight up, at least talk to me." I shift to bring some feeling back into my ass. One cut has stopped bleeding, but the other three still trickle over my waist. "Why killing? What made you want to do this?"

She looks at me, contemplating whether or not she wants to answer. Despite the circumstances, I can tell that she kind of likes me. It's a liking that I'm sure confuses her. This has been the basis for a lot of my friendships.

"My entire life," she finally says, "involves saving people through very controlled, precise rules."

I raise my eyebrows at her, and she continues, "I really am a nurse. I didn't lie about that. Hell, where do you think I got all this stuff?" She holds up her purse, the source of the rag, the scrubs, the scalpel, and I hope to God nothing else. "It's a profession that found me. All day I'm surrounded by the threat of death, and it's my job to stop it. I always have to stop it. Even when there's no hope."

She sighs, losing her coldness. "It wears on you. I'm supposed to make dying people better. All day I'm covered in blood, in shit and vomit and disease. I have people yell and scream at me, even though I'm trying to help them live. Sometimes in the chaos, I find myself thinking, what if I did the exact opposite of what I'm supposed to do?"

A small smile seeps across her face. "At first I'd simply imagine mistakes here and there. A slipped scalpel. A fatal medication dose. It's so easy to kill someone in a place that's meant to help people. It's really fascinating, if you think about it. Almost thrilling."

Her eyes are looking away from me now, and I can see her imagining every patient she's treated dying a horrible death. I recognize that look, the one of macabre possibility that only killers possess. I get that look every time I imagine taking someone apart. "You seem like a wonderful nurse," I murmur.

Her attention returns to me. "I actually studied nursing to try to curb that thrill," she explains. "My whole life, I've had fantasies about slipping up, of breaking the rules. What-if scenarios where I'd break something, make it irreversible. Where I'd hurt someone, and they'd never recover." She returns her gaze to me. "Where I'd kill someone, and they'd never come back. I thought maybe if I devoted myself to helping people, I'd stop thinking about ways to hurt them."

Her blade touches my chest, and I feel my pulse quicken. "But I was wrong. It only made it worse. It made me want to do it even more." She looks back at me, holding my eyes with a cold stare. "And it taught me how to do it more effectively."

She makes a quick swipe across my chest. I cry in pain, watching fresh blood spill over. It's always just enough to hurt and bleed, but not to make me pass out or find sweet relief in death. I'm sure she knows that. It's all on purpose.

"So you've done this a lot," I say, talking through the pain.

"Actually, no," she says, chuckling. "Congratulations — you're my first victim."

Of course I am. "Great. I feel so special."

"You should." She runs her hand over my cut, tracing blood over my skin. "You're leaving a mark on me, just like I'm leaving them on you. I'll never forget you."

"Awesome. I'm so fucking flattered." I'd love nothing more than to snap off her hand and shove it up her ass right now.

"I just can't believe I bested you in so many ways on my first try. I got to you before you got to me." Her

51

leer turns into a grin. "And, I got to make my first kill before you."

Little does she know.

The term "serial killer" implies multiple killings and patterned murders. In this sense, I am not a serial killer. I'd hoped to be, but I didn't meet that criteria.

This is not to say, though, that I am not a killer. That only requires one murder.

My life has always been pretty unremarkable. Well-off parents, reasonably adjusted childhood. I some-times wonder if my killer instincts subconsciously came from wanting to break up the monotony. All I know is that, at a pretty young age, I stopped seeing people and started seeing their parts.

I still remember the first time this happened. I'd watch my teacher in school, and entertain myself by imagining her head floating off her body, her hands suspended in the air still writing on the chalkboard, and her feet tapping silently under the desk. Then one day I imagined taking those pieces apart myself — rip-ping them off, and placing them one-by-one around the classroom. I quickly squelched that fantasy. It was wrong to think that.

I never hurt anyone when I was young. I still lis-tened to adults, people on TV who sent criminals to jail for hurting people. They said that hurting people was wrong. But seeing them in pieces never really went away. It came and went in flickers. I'd do it with strang-ers, with actors in movies. Kept it at a distance.

I toyed with having those thoughts about my friends. If the thoughts arose, I quickly banished them. Strangers only. No one close. But they kept popping up, and after a while, I let myself have them, if only to make myself feel the horror that came with them. It shocked me to think of my friend's head lying on a carving block. It frightened me to imagine my girlfriend's pussy dissolving over my hand while I fingered her.

I grew concerned when those thoughts stopped being repulsive. I became a little more concerned when I started thinking them intentionally.

Soon, though, they became an escape. Things around me could spin chaotically — my friend could die of cancer, my girlfriend could leave me, people could come and go and school could wear on me and jobs could suck, but I could take it all apart in my mind. It was the only place I could do that, and sometimes, it was the only place I could feel content.

Those fantasies were comforting because they gave me some illusion of control. I could decide if someone lived or died. I could prove to their bodies that I could control their fate. Bodies were too taken with themselves. They could disappear just as easily as they could stand, walk, or talk. I could take them apart, or I could leave them alone. What would it be?

I never fully withdrew, but it did become harder and harder to not imagine the people I spoke to lying in pieces. I shouldn't hurt them. I wouldn't hurt them.

But oh, how I wanted to.

My parents both died suddenly. They were in a car accident. When I heard the news, I didn't even cry. I imagined their car tearing through their bodies. One minute whole, the next in pieces. I only saw their pieces, as they were cremated as soon as I identified them. I never touched them, never took them myself. Something else taken away from me.

One night, a few weeks after they'd died, I went out driving. I drove past the strip malls, the gas stations, the lone Wal-Mart. I wondered how far I could go before I left people behind forever, and how much further I could go before finding them again.

Almost in answer, my eyes chanced upon someone walking ahead on the road. They were walking away from me, strolling casually on the side of the road, as if they did this every day. I only saw them because their white shoes and vinyl jacket shimmered in my headlights. They were alone. Their back was turned to me. They walked as if nothing could hurt them — as if they were in complete control.

I'd show them.

I sped up and jerked the steering wheel to the left. I don't even know if they knew I was coming. They never turned around, not until I'd already hit them. And even then, they didn't turn around so much as land on the hood of my car.

They — or he, as I then saw — ricocheted to the side, and I slammed on the brakes. I turned around, saw him lying on the road.

I ran over him again.

I did it once more for good measure.

I put the car in park. He lay on the road, not moving. I'd killed someone. I'd finally done it.

I looked in my rearview mirror, and saw him staying still. He had to be dead. No one would survive being run over three times.

But I had to make sure. I had to control this.

I got out of the car, scooped up his broken body, and placed him in my trunk, his arms crumpling under his torso. As luck would have it, I had some plastic garbage bags back there. It'd make clean-up easier. But where could I take him?

I continued driving forward, figuring these woods would do me well. These woods. They seemed pretty familiar. I drove by a sign with a couple town names. Meadow Rush and Thatcher's Hill. Nature names that probably described some pretty places, but nowhere anyone would actually live. But Meadow Rush rang a bell.

We'll see you next week, son. We're going to the cabin out in Meadow Rush.

The cabin. Mom and Dad had a cabin in the middle of nowhere. I'd gone with them for a month one summer and hated every day of it, but they adored it. It had been their private getaway, a place where they'd go to escape people for a while. Mom would go out there alone and write. Dad would go there and hunt. And as far as I knew, it still stood, unaware that its beloved patrons were reduced to ash and buried closer to civilization.

Fortunately, I now remembered where it was. I turned down a couple of side streets and drove deeper into the woods, until the trees suddenly cleared and there it was.

I got out of the car and looked around. There wasn't a soul for miles. It really was the middle of nowhere. I was amazed there was even electricity. Trees stretched in every direction beyond the clearing, carved only by the road connecting the driveway to the main road. A lone vein to the heart of humanity. Could I sever that too?

I checked to see if the spare keys were in the same place. Sure enough, there they were, under the fake log by the porch. I pocketed them, and opened the trunk. My victim was still motionless, still breathless. I picked him up, his arm hanging limply over mine as I carried him to the cabin.

Inside, it was musty and quiet. I flicked on the light, and saw everything that had made the place a home away from home for my parents. Furniture, an ancient computer, lamps. The bedroom door was open, and I saw a fully-made bed with a linen cabinet next to it. I laid the body on the floor and walked around, finding signs of my parents but no one else. The only sounds around me were crickets, toads, and the occasional bird. There wasn't a soul for miles. I was alone.

Well, not completely alone.

I looked back at the body. It lay in a heap of plastic. He was dead, and I needed to make sure he'd never be found. There were the floorboards. I could just leave him in the cabin, maybe burn this place to the ground or something.

As I thought, my eyes continued scanning the cabin and found the kitchen. They stopped upon a full knife set. I paused, then walked over to it. Despite a light layer of dust, they were in pristine condition.

I returned to the living room with a meat cleaver. He lay on the floor, dead. Was he dead? I was sure he was dead. I had to make sure he was dead.

I could make sure he was dead.

I could control this.

I imagined taking him apart, piece by piece. I imagined burying the parts in precise locations. I could make a pattern, one that spelled out the make of my car or some other clue.

I imagined him broken and buried. And I didn't even try to blink it away. I didn't remind myself that this was wrong. Because here, it wasn't. Here, there was no one for it to be wrong to. There was nobody here — and as such, I could hide anybody in any way that I wanted.

I smiled.

I smiled.

"Why are you smiling?"

I'm staring at the ceiling. I bring myself back to Candace, to the present. I look down and see I'm still bleeding.

"No reason," I say. I won't give her the satisfaction of my own background. "Just remembering things."

I had decided that night that the cabin would be my home, and that killing would be my new normal. It was the only normal I could keep.

But even that hadn't worked out. I never wanted to leave the cabin, since it was the perfect place to hide. I never saw anything in the news about a missing man. I hid anyway, just in case. I made small trips at night to clear out some essential stuff from my apartment, but otherwise, I abandoned what I had before so I could fully become what I'd always been.

The initial thrill, however, wore off when I realized victims wouldn't just fall in my lap. I had to find them. But I didn't want to. Until I did.

And now I'm here.

I still remember how I felt after that first kill. Years of confusion, suppression, and chaos had been set in order at last. I finally had the control that I craved, that I longed to demonstrate, that I was eager to show others. But I couldn't do that when there was no one around.

And that was the ultimate problem. I couldn't control bodies that weren't there. I had to go to them. And even when I went to them, I couldn't necessarily control what they did to me. Tonight is clear evidence of that.

Maybe tonight is that man's retribution. Maybe I'm learning a cruel lesson about life by losing my own. Maybe it's happening because it's happening and there's absolutely nothing I can do about it. Whatever the reason, I know one thing for sure: I lost.

"Hey!" Candace smacks my leg. Zoning out has become less voluntary. Maybe the blood loss is finally catching up with me. I blink and make eye contact with her, show her I'm still alive — even if not for much longer.

"What?" I manage. "Why do you even want me conscious right now?" Couldn't she just kill me?

"I only want you unconscious," she says, "when I make the right cut."

"So make it," I say, closing my eyes. "I've got nothing to say to you."

I feel her grab my hair and lift up my head. I open my eyes, and she's glaring at me. "I'll make it when I'm ready," she says. "I make the rules."

"No, you don't." I gain enough of a second wind to furrow my brow and speak through clenched teeth. "You think you do, but you don't."

"What are you talking about?" She keeps her grip on my hair.

I know I'm talking to myself more than her, but I don't care. "The rules. You think you've made them, or broken them, or made them by breaking them. You haven't. You got me, but because I came to you. You'll kill me, and leave me here, and feel like a success. You can see it all ahead of you, one kill after the other to counter your stupid job. But you don't know what will happen next. You don't know if the cops will find me or find you. You don't know if the person you find next will do the exact same thing to you. You don't know the rules, because in the end, there aren't any. You don't know anything!"

I use my ever-dwindling strength to spit at her. It lands on her face, and she barely flinches. She calmly wipes her face, keeping eye contact with me.

"You're right," she says. Not what I was expecting. It's a running theme this evening. "I don't know what will happen after this. Everyone thinks they know what will happen, that if they do X and Y, that Z will happen. But that's bullshit."

We're so much alike. Maybe in another life, we could've worked together.

"I watch people die every day, people who did X and Y and expected Z, but got something else entirely." She twirls the scalpel against her finger. "They expect me to give them Z. And I have to try my hardest to do so."

She leans towards me. "But not here. Not now. Here and now, I can give whatever answer I want. Here and now, I not only know the answer …" The scalpel leaves her finger, floats to my arm. "… I determine it."

She smiles. "And it feels great."

She makes a sudden slash. I look over and see a long, cascading cut crawling up my entire arm. Blood starts pouring out immediately. As the sight sinks in, she turns and does the same to my other arm. Both cuts long and vertical. Both slashing their respective veins. Both marking the end.

I cry in pain, but that's about the only amount of panic I can muster. I lie helpless, watching my arms drain. Watch her watching me, still smiling. She gets off of me, and stands by my side. She runs a palm through my hair, keeps it on my head. Strokes me. "Shh," she says. "It'll be over soon."

I look ahead. I don't want her to see inside me as I die.

I remember the first time I fell asleep in this cabin, during that month from hell with my parents. My heart had raced when the lights went out. I'd never been surrounded by that much darkness. It was suffocating. I'd held my hand in front of me, and couldn't even see it. I knew what blindness felt like. I felt trapped under a blanket, one I could claw and tear at, but never rip away.

Now though, I don't panic. I see that blanket as a comfort. The bleeding, Candace's stare, her cuts, the pieces, the loneliness — it'll all be over soon. It'll all be shut out by this darkness, one I now fully embrace.

I close my eyes.

He's gone.

I keep my eyes on him as I grab some rubbing alcohol, pouring it over the scalpel to clean it. He doesn't move, he doesn't breathe. He's no longer here. He's gone — and I took him away.

I smile. All in a night's work.

I leave him tied up. I use his shower. Air-dry instead of using a towel. I've left enough evidence of my presence without adding more. I debate doing a complete scrub-down of the place, but part of me wants to leave clues. More of me also knows no one will ever come looking for him.

I put my bar clothes back on, walking through the various places where I shed them. He was one of the best fucks I've ever had. A shame I'd already decided on his fate. Maybe in another life, we could've lived out here, fucking and killing together. It wouldn't be the worst life. But it wasn't in the cards. Not this time.

My medical supplies are back in my purse. The scrubs I'm not sure what to do with. They're covered in his blood. Laundry will only do so much.

I consider his fireplace, then feel the floor wiggle beneath me as I move towards it. Of course — the floorboards. A classic hiding place, and one without the presence of smoke to draw attention. I'll leave them there. No one will find them. No one else has been here.

I lift up the board, and see that I'm mistaken.

Lying underneath of the board is a single, decomposing arm. It still has much of its skin, the fingers gnarled with death. A bit of cloth from a shirt remains. Enclosed by the bit of cloth is an open wound, which is crawling with maggots.

I'm smacked by both the sight and the stench of it, and slam the board back into place. I press the board down further with my foot, hoping that's enough to keep the bugs, smell, and as silly as it is, the arm from resurfacing.

He hadn't died victimless — he'd gotten someone. Maybe he got multiple someones.

He could've gotten me.

My heartbeat begins to climb. Part of me thought he was just bullshitting when he said he was going to kill me — that he was just scared, or trying to scare me. But his words, the isolated cabin, and most of all the severed arm confirm he wasn't bluffing.

I think about all the times I could've died tonight. The minute we left in his car and drove far away, where no one would see who we were or what we did. As soon as we walked into the cabin, me letting him put his hands wherever he wanted on my body. I remember catching a glimpse at his kitchen while he was going down on me, and seeing that collection of knives. I didn't think for one second he'd use them for anything except meal preparation. I didn't think he'd do anything on his bed except sleep and fuck.

I look in the direction of the bed and jump at the sight of him.

Dead. He's still dead. Of course he's dead. I've killed him.

I shudder, thinking he could just as easily killed me, and keep telling myself that he didn't. I killed him. I dismantled his paint-by-numbers night, injected my own chaos. I won.

Did I?

I can't dwell on it now. I straighten my shoulders, getting myself together. I stuff my scrubs in a plastic bag lying near the kitchen. I'll burn them at home. I do a quick glance through the cabin, looking for any remaining things. I take one final look at him. Still tied up, still covered in blood. Still dead. I hope he'll stay that way.

I grab his car keys from the shelf by the door and make a swift exit. The car will also need to be disposed of, but I'll take care of that later.

I climb in the car and rev the engine, trying not to peel away too quickly. The last thing I want to do is wreck the car before I even get on the highway. I take one final glimpse of the place that almost held me forever, the final resting place of the man who almost got me. The perfect place to leave the body.

ACKNOWLEDGMENTS

This collection was made possible by two particular people:

Evelyn Duffy, my editor. Thank you for the work you did to bring these pieces into better form.

Doug Puller, the cover artist. I appreciate the life you breathed into this collection with your artwork.

Many thanks as well to my friends who read these stories in their earliest forms, and provided feedback and ideas to help shape them. Writing is a team effort between author and reader, and I'm lucky to have such wonderful teammates.

Thank you for reading.

Photo by Karen Papadales

ABOUT THE AUTHOR

Sonora Taylor is the author of *The Crow's Gift and Other Tales* and *Please Give*. She lives in Arlington, Virginia, with her husband.

Visit her online at sonorawrites.com

Made in the USA
Middletown, DE
27 April 2021

38121849R00045